# A very Red Hood Rising
## Krampusmas

By Katelynn Alexandrea
This book contains public domain characters, a
deity, Saint Nicholas, a dragon, and a continuation
of zero copyright infringements.

# Happy Sintaklaas!

Sintaklaas has always had a special place in our family's hearts with special thanks to my mother, so quite obviously;

## For Momsje

And, of course

## Jared Padelecki(Mom's favorite), and Jensen Ackles

(Mom's favorite huntsmen seemed appropriate.)

# Frosting and sirens

Contrary to popular belief, "Frosted Siren" comes from cake frosting, and not a fondness for cold. I don't especially LIKE winter, and I'm not overly fond of being cold, either.

Holiday thanks go out to everyone who makes the season bright;

Jess, or as you know her, Cinderella. Our worlds my be veiled apart, but I appreciate everything.

The usual joy bringers; Mom, Shashy, Claira, All the other Jess's, Ellie, Pixie, Cookie, Sephi, Toast, Bob, Lexie(And Lexie), Sunny, and Juffy.

Thanks also to Minerrale, artist extraordinaire, and the quartet of spirit lifters, Doctors Z and N, Editor dad and Villain dad.

Thanks to Sintaklaas for all the oranges, and Santa for somehow deciding I didn't deserve coal when I was growing up.

And of course,

**You, for buying this book.**
*With wishes of joy and light, I would not be able to do what I do without readers like you. Thank you so much.*

# Silent night

## (Prologue)

# The reclaimed land

The Netherlands were not *German*, but that's not to say they weren't *Germanic* in origin.

A beautiful place. The mills were powered by the winds instead of the rivers. There wasn't a place quite like the Beemer polders in all of Europa.

Eleanor said that she wanted to see something so far removed from anything she had ever seen in Perrault that she would not believe it was real.

This scene was it. We sat on one of the dikes, watching as the citizens went about their day.

The windmills slowly drained the lake that was previously part of the ocean. They milled grains grown in the land reclaimed by the windmills.

We could smell the bread already. There was still maybe an hour to walk.

The snow was just starting to fall. The chill set in, and we both wrapped our cloaks a bit closer around ourselves.

I had never done this before. It was not a thing that people in my profession got to do.

I had never been *on a vacation*. I had tried, sure, but it was never successful.

Eleanor sat next to me sipping from her water canteen. She smiled peacefully.

"I'll give you this much." She said, staring out at the windmills with awe. "This is definitely the most fantastic thing I've ever seen."

"They make some of the best cheeses you can get your hands on, too." I reached into my bag to withdraw some of my leftover food. "Which is good." I paused to look at my last remaining helping of dried carrion bird. "I've got silver, but an empty bag of food."

"I still cannot believe you know how to cook this. What do you call these things again?" Eleanor looked into her own makeshift bag, and frowned. "I'm almost out, too."

"Mouette." I paused. "Though, in the language I was raised to speak, we called them Gulls of the Sea."

"I must admit that the assortment of food one eats while travelling alongside you is… exotic." Eleanor's tone was quite dry.

"Listen, it keeps you fed." I couldn't help but chuckle. "Unfortunately, we've run out of landscape suitable for foraging, and the birds aren't interested in coming close enough. You eat what you can."

Eleanor looked out towards the water, thoughtfully. "Could you not fish?"

I shook my head. "I'm afraid that's a very dangerous water to fish in. Voyaging on the ocean is quite expensive, and hazardous."

"The ocean?" She scrunched up her face. "Aren't there… monsters in the ocean?"

"Depends on your definition of monster." I tilted my head. "You know, I've been meaning to try this."

"Try what?" She gave me a confused look.

I put my cloak down, and slowly undressed, revealing bows, arrows, knives, swords, and some strange potions.

I looked at my empty food bag, and then back at Eleanor.

"We're going to eat well, tonight, before heading into town." I winked.

Eleanor looked out at the ocean.

She gave a delighted look.

"I forgot." She admitted, with a shake of her head. "That's where you belong."

"Oh, no." I paused, to give her a wink. "I belong right here, with you."

I took a moment to stare out at the ocean again, before taking a deep breath.

"This is just a temporary delight." I added.

"Safe hunting, Rachel."

"Fair winds, and following seas is the way we wish sailors luck where I am from."

"You aren't a sailor."

"Fair point."

# Windmills and cheese wheels

With full bellies, and cured fish in our bags, we began the walk towards Beemster the following morning.

The walk was brisk, and the snow crunched under our feet.

Eleanor watched the townsfolk with curiosity.

"Is something wrong, here?" She asked. "Are you here for work?"

"What makes you say that?" I asked, my interest piqued by her observation.

"The townsfolk are hushed. Secretive. Look. The markets are quiet. Normally it should be a buzz, this early in the morning." She frowned, and gestured. "The market stalls are quiet. Even the merchants have closed up early."

I looked up at the sun, trying to gauge the time, then my concern started to set in.

"It's deserted." My hands went to my sword, and I closed the distance between myself and Eleanor, handing her my offhand sword.

"What?" She took it, frowning. "You know I'm still not very good with this."

"Eleanor, hush." I twirled my blade, getting myself stretched for what I expected would be trouble.

Someone approached but they didn't appear to be a threat, despite having a weapon of their own.

"Welcome to Beemster." The man noted, tilting his head.

He spoke in Dutch. Eleanor didn't understand Dutch. She frowned, taking a defensive stance.

I lowered my weapon.

Eleanor took my cue and did the same.

"A curious welcome." I replied, though my Dutch was not high in the top 10 list of languages I had a rough understanding of. "It's not even close to midday, and the shops are closed. We're quite tired from our travels."

"As it so happens, we don't get travellers very often." The guard inclined his head. "Come along. The inn is much kinder. The warmth is also a benefit."

"Warmth, we'll take. Ale would be excellent, as well." I nodded towards the guard, switching to French. "He says he'll lead us to the inn. There's a fire, and food."

"Well, THAT is a proper welcome." Eleanor placed the sword awkwardly in the sheath I had readjusted so she could wear. She was a lot more slight than most swordspeople, and it took some handiwork that grandma would have been proud of.

"Your companion seems new to that." The guard noted, idly.

"She is. I'm not." I retorted. "It's my profession, actually."

"A mercenary?" The guard asked.

"A woods' woman." I replied. "That isn't right. Sorry. I speak quite new in this language."

"And she, not at all." He nodded. "A woods' woman? Is that anything like a Huntsman?"

I winced. The word was in a Nordic pronunciation. It was a bit jarring at the end of the dutch sentence. "Exactly." I paused. "Though

I prefer Huntswoman."

"Didn't think your kind traveled so close to each other." The Guard paused. "Though you don't look the-" He froze, and turned to look me over.

"What?" I looked around. "Are we here?"

"The red cloak." He pointed at me. "Are you-"

"Rachel." I interjected. "You don't want to call me that."

"Did he say the thing?" Eleanor asked, looking concerned.

"My apologies, miss. This way." He nodded. "The bards sang strange songs about wolves."

"I would be very shocked if they got it right." I shook my head. "Unpleasant subject."

The guard tilted his head, before nodding and opening the door. "They do that. It is not kind."

The townsfolk all turned to see who was coming in.

And sitting at the end of the table was an improbably large man with an even more improbably sized axe sitting next to him.

"Who is that?" Eleanor asked.

"Well, I'll be damned." I muttered.

"What?" Eleanor frowned. "Is he… dangerous?"

"Of course he is." I laughed. "He's a huntsman."

"Fair." Eleanor didn't find this comforting. "Do you know who he is?'

"Oh, yes." I shook my head. "He's a legend. I just didn't realize he was real. Or still alive."

I approached the man, and took a seat next to him.

"Hood." He said, quietly.

"Klaas." I quirked an eyebrow. I hadn't expected him to know who I was. "Eleanor Tremaine, may I introduce Nicholas Klaas, nordic huntsman of impressive legends."

"A pleasure to meet you, Sir Nicholas." Eleanor offered a slight curtsey.

The man laughed. "I'm about as much a sir as your companion is a lady."

Eleanor tried not to laugh.

"What brings you two to this cold, damp, unpleasant place?" He turned to me, with a stern glare.

"Eleanor has never been outside a small French village before now." I paused. "We weren't really looking for trouble."

"Though it tends to find her." Eleanor added.

"Such is the way of our life." Nicholas nodded. "As it so happens-"

I sighed. "I go where there's trouble."

"And fix it." Nicholas agreed. "For the right price."

"What's the price on this one?" Eleanor asked.

Nicholas nodded his head in the direction of a group of kids playing quietly in the corner.

"Peace." He said, quietly.

"Doesn't sound like it pays a lot." Eleanor scrunched up her face.

"For children?" I shook my head. "That's payment enough."

"What is?" She suddenly fell quiet.

"The chance that they won't live the life we had to live." I said, quietly. "Welcome to the guild of Huntsmen, Eleanor Tremaine."

Nicholas chuckled at that, and patted Eleanor's back. "You're one of us, then?"

Eleanor looked at the children, and then nodded. "As Rachel puts it, Huntsmen are rarely made of warm hearths, and full bellies."

"Peace." Nicholas raised his mug. "That's something beyond gold or silver."

"Not unlike other treasures one is fortunate enough to have in their life." I added.

Eleanor brightened. "So. What are we saving them from?"

"I'm gonna like her." Nicholas put his hand on his stomach, before letting out a hearty laugh. "Saving them? This thing can't be killed."

"I've yet to come across anything I couldn't kill if I was really determined about it." I retorted.

"Spoken like a proper huntsman."

"Huntswoman."

# Ho ho ho, who wouldn't know?

(Act one)

# The Anti-Klaas

It took quite some time for proper food and ale to be prepared for us, though the innkeeper was happy to oblige. Paying customers were rarely considered unwelcome in any tavern.

Nikolaas and Eleanor were both quiet as the fire was brought a bit warmer, and they both apparently needed it.

I wasn't as bothered by the cold as others. Likely a part of my *condition*.

After a table was set for us, Nikolaas placed a lantern on the table, and withdrew some scraps of rags with an unfamiliar language written on it.

"What is that?" Eleanor asked, tilting her head at the rag.

"Scraps." Nikolaas paused. "From what I've gathered, this thing always hunts on a specific day of the year. It is a bit harder to gauge in some places because the winter solstice isn't a concern. Precisely 16 days before the solstice, it abducts children, and then it is done. Can't find a trace of it for another year."

"How do you know it's not some normal forest creature or bog thing?" Eleanor's face scrunched up as she asked the question.

"Nature eats when it's hungry, girl. Only monsters follow such strict rules as this. Were it a beast, or wild thing, it would happen more regularly, and in smaller abductions." Nikolaas paused. "And as near as anyone can tell, it only specifically targets problematic children."

"Humans follow rules like that." Eleanor looked down. "With annual balls, and harvest festivals."

Nikolaas gave her a nod. "I said precisely what I meant." He paused to take a swig of his drink. "Though that is an excellent observation."

"What observation?" Eleanor frowned.

"You suggested that this may just as easily be man as monster." I interjected, before stuffing my mouth with more of the delightful bread I had been smelling for days.

Eleanor blinked before looking back at Nikolaas. "How would that work, though?"

"All the right questions, girl." Nikolaas chuckled. "Barkeep, another!" He threw the wooden mug to the ground with such force that it bounced back into the air.

I grabbed it out of the air and hissed. "They don't do that here." I grabbed my own mug and went to get a refill, nodding to the inn keep. "My apologies. My friend is…"

"Exuberant." The Innkeep laughed. "Why do you think he gets the wooden plates and mugs?" He added, before refilling both mugs.

I left him a few coins and we exchanged a nod.

Returning my focus to Eleanor and Nikolaas, it was fascinating to see how quickly she had adapted to this life, and how we had to think for it.

"So." Eleanor held up a finger. "It could not possibly travel that distance in one night without magic, and it targets specific behavior, abducts them, and then vanishes for a full year."

Nikolaas nodded. "And no normal person nor creature could pull that off."

"It hunts with something called soul reading." I interjected, as I put the mugs before us. "Fairies use it." I added, pausing to take a sip. "Everything you do or don't do changes how magical creatures perceive you. Some don't even see how you look to other humans. As such, this creature is specifically targeting children who offend it in some way."

Eleanor blinked. "Can you do that?"

Nikolaas focused his attention intently on me after that question.

I shook my head. "Neither with my present curse, nor most of the ones I've suffered prior. Be they vampiric, werewolf, or siren, the senses are transformed into that of the beast you've been cursed to represent."

Nikolaas narrowed his eyes. "And what senses do you use, now, girl?"

"*Rachel*." I retorted. "And her name is Eleanor." I took a moment to recollect my anger. He was deliberately attempting to bait me into replying as a beast, rather than as a woman. "I was cursed into being a siren by a forest witch."

"Makes sense. You'd have a hard time wielding the things that could kill her because they could harm you, as well." He paused. "And in the middle of the forest, even if she lost, she'd have left the forests angry with you. Fish don't belong above the water."

"In the future." Eleanor took a quick and mousey bite of her bread. "You should probably be aware that she's spent more of her life cursed than not. Trying to aggravate her like that isn't a smart idea."

Nikolaas stared at us both for some moments, before tearing into a leg of boar. He was silent while he chewed, regarding us with a strange expression. Then, he nodded. "She is a child of magic, but that does not make her nefarious."

"I can be, should I be so provoked." I retorted.

Nikolaas flashed a smile at that. "That is precisely the spirit you're going to need if we're seriously going to hunt this thing."

"Why is that?" Eleanor regarded his change of attitude towards us with a defensive position, which only made him smile further.

"You have good instincts, Eleanor." He paused. "And yours, I imagine, are instilled by varying curses. Wolf Child, yes? I believe I have heard the tale many times."

I bared my less human teeth at him with an angry expression.

"Ah. Not a fan of that." He chuckled. "Well then, Rachel Hunter Siren." He regarded Eleanor. "And Eleanor Mouse Warrior." He inclined his head. "I am Nikolaas White Beard, an honorific title unusual to our line of work."

"In what way?" Eleanor pondered. "And how do you know about my affinity for mice?"

"Hunstmen don't tend to grow old." I shook my head. "Which means he is either very skilled at what he does, or smart enough to know when he isn't skilled enough."

"A skill you lack." Eleanor retorted, slightly amused.

"Do not be so quick to dismiss." Nikolaas shook his head. "She chooses a proper huntsman's path. She is willing to lay down her life for ones such as they." He gestured to the children in the corner. "Or you. When you arrived here, I told you that this was not a creature you could hunt. As to the mice, I have noticed you attempting to feed them without drawing attention."

"They were my only friend for a time, so I'll grant you that one.. Rachel immediately decided she was going to hunt it, despite your warnings." She reached out for my hand.

"I hunt that which I know I can hunt, and I have grown old and fat." He paused. "She hunts things in such a way that she doesn't care if she can, or can not. It isn't about her ability. It's about the necessity of the job. How many curses have you suffered for the good of others?"

"Werewolfism thrice, vampirism once. I turned into a tree during the day for a few years, and I also had the great misfortune of being forced to marry a prince so that he would not execute some villagers who helped a hero try to overthrow him." She paused. "That's where Hood comes from."

"As in *Robin*?" Nikolaas paused, then shook his head. "I see."

"And now she is a siren." Eleanor added.

"And for what reason did you go to kill the witch that cursed you?" Nikolaas implored.

"She had cursed the village. If you called someone a pig, they'd become one. Slips of the tongue, or common sayings caused mass chaos. I never did figure out why. She didn't give me the chance." I paused. "They were just quiet backwater people, trying to live."

"And that is why we are the way we are." Nikolaas paused. "Sometimes, when people are hurt, they turn to such things as anger, or witchcraft, or the power of being a prince, and they cause harm. Sometimes they do not."

"And just as people turn to that villainy." I raised my mug. "Huntsmen are made of the same stuff. We just use it to help others."

"Hurt people often hurt other people." Nikolaas clinked his mug against mine. "That doesn't make us right. That doesn't make them wrong. It does not give them the right to ruin an entire village's life."

"Nor to steal children simply because they haven't lived long enough to learn the lessons that stop them from acting like a bratty child." Eleanor added.

"And thus, we arrive at your friend's line of hunting." Nikolaas clinked his mug against hers. "You're a quick study. I can see why she brought you along."

"Oh, trust me." I paused to squeeze Eleanor's hand. "That had very little to do with it."

"Ah." Nikolaas shook his head. "Sirens. No matter." He chuckled a bit. "The concept of relative harm, or appropriate justice for a wrong is a grayscale in our life. Sometimes, it's a goldscale. Sometimes a silverscale."

"Sometimes, it's a curse cure ingredient." I interjected.

"Quite so." He took a moment to thoughtfully stare into his drink. "I would imagine that would get tedious after the third or fourth curse."

"Not if you start curing curses with curses." I shrugged.

"Particularly if you replace a curse with a curse you can cure." Eleanor ripped off some of her bread so that she could chew it easier. "Supposedly this curse can't be undone that way."

Nikolaas contemplated his drink a while more, while we ate a bit in silence.

"Relative harm." He added. "Also relates to whom they are harming. Targeting children who don't know better or are simply being children." He sighed heavily. "I have lived so long ignoring creatures such as this."

"I don't believe in such luxuries as ignorance on that scale." I retorted.

He stared at me intensely for several moments. "You couldn't live with doing nothing." He nodded. "We shall make for a larger city in the morning."

"Why?" Eleanor blinked, surprised by this seemingly out of place remark.

"Larger cities mean more children. More children mean more children who misbehave." I took the discarded crusts of her bread and traded them for some of the fruit on my plate which didn't agree with siren stomachs. "If we are to devise a trap, or attempt a hunt, it is always best to use the most bait."

"They are children." Eleanor looked at me with a disapproving look.

"And without our help, they will be dead." I retorted. "Morality like that is a luxury. I don't particularly believe in that, either."

"In this line of work, there is a monster, a way to track it, and a way to kill it. The faster you do the last two, the less damage it can do." Nikolaas agreed.

"Then why not head out tonight?" Eleanor grumbled.

"Can't get a boat nor wagon to travel those roads at night." Nikolaas shrugged. "Monsters, right?" He asked the Innkeeper.

"Kabouter. Draeck. Wild dogs." The Innkeeper paused. "Lange Wapper, probably. The world goes mad after the fall harvests."

I took a moment to translate his words for Eleanor.

"Monsters?" Eleanor paused. "Let me get this straight, famed monster hunter of legend." She pointed an accusatory finger. "You won't leave tonight because there may be monsters on the road?"

"Rachel did not use the right word." Nikolaas retorted. "*Draeck* is the Dutch word for *Dragon*."

"So?" Eleanor glared. "A monster such as that plaguing these people and you do *nothing*?"

"Never meet the legends the bards tell." I grumbled. "It would seem that the helpless Wolf Child is far less a coward than the famed viking monster hunter of the south."

Nikolaas looked indignant.

"We have full bellies, and sharp swords." I handed the innkeeper some extra coins. "We leave now."

"This is too much." The innkeeper said, looking at the coins.

"You always thank those who find you work." I retorted. "I'm sure there are plenty who would pay to see such creatures taken down."

"Well, obviously." The innkeeper paused. "Though it will be hard to be paid if you are dead, or worse. The Kabouter do not treat those who see them kindly."

"And I'm a huntswoman." I retorted. "I assure you that the inverse is true, should they threaten people simply trying to make their way."

"Girl, you will get you and her both killed." Nikolaas now had an angry tone.

"Her name is Rachel." Eleanor paused. "And if we die, we die helping people."

"A better death, the world doesn't offer." I added.

Nikolaas shook his head. "Alright, fine. Far be it for ones so slightly as you to accuse me of cowardice when you do so correctly."

# The unforgiving night

The silence surrounding us as we began our travel to the south east was quite unnerving. The wind would occasionally ruffle the trees. The sounds of forest creatures skittering away from perceived threats. Rabbits. Deer. Foxes.

On a cold winter eve like this, their footsteps were thankfully not echoed in the woods. The snow acted as a sound dampener. That had its misgivings. It was far easier for things to sneak through the world around us, unseen.

The woods around us regarded us with a great deal of distress. Nikolaas and I both appeared to offend the way the world was supposed to be, though it had little interest in Eleanor. Magic did that. As did things outside the natural order.

This intrigued me, and as we walked, I focused my attention on the nature around us. How the woods spoke to each other. What they said. Why they feared him.

They offered no explanation beyond their fear. This wasn't unusual. It was frustrating, however. The world did not speak as humans did. It spoke in subtleties.

It still set me on guard around him.

And then I was assaulted by a scent ahead of us. I stopped short. Eleanor stopped quickly after.

"Don't." She whispered to Nikolaas, breaking our group silence.

Nikolaas paused, turning his attention to me.

In the dark, siren eyes and scents were far more of use than human ones, but it did not take him long to understand.

"That's smoke." He said, softly. "Fire."

The forest became hushed, but the fleeing of creatures made it obvious. The fire was in the direction we were headed.

This knowledge set me further on edge. I bared my teeth in the dark, annoyed.

"Easy." Eleanor said, grabbing my hand.

I shook my head. "This fire is wrong."

"Not to mention a natural predator of sirens like yourself." Nikolaas added. "Her response is appropriate."

"Right." Eleanor winced. "When you're in the wild, it's a lot safer to trust the instincts of the wild around you."

"Ah. She has taught you already." Nikolaas nodded. "It would be important, I imagine."

"I forget, sometimes." Eleanor admitted.

"Well, wildling." Nikolaas looked out at the woods ahead of us. "Do we go forward, or not?"

"Is there another way?" Eleanor asked.

"It will take longer." Nikolaas looked towards me. "That's why I'm asking her."

There was something in the air. A scent. Something that did not belong in a wildfire.

*Demon. Monster.*

I grabbed my sword and wordlessly walked forward.

"Ah." Nikolaas chuckled. "I see."

"She is stubborn." Eleanor shrugged. She withdrew her sword and followed me cautiously.

Nikolaas grabbed his axe, and nodded. "Well, if we die, we die doing what's right, I suppose."

Something in the air made a terrifyingly overpowering noise.

I looked in the direction it came from and bared my teeth. Eleanor covered her ears.

Nikolaas did not.

I shrieked angrily at the thing in the dark.

Nikolaas staggered back.

Eleanor uncovered her ears. "Get ready."

"What?" Nikolaas asked.

"I said get ready!" Eleanor shouted.

"I can't-" Nikolaas began.

Something grabbed him from the sky and he was gone.

"Well." Eleanor winced.

"Get down." I began rushing towards her.

She ducked down into the snow.

I screamed again.

The thing made its noise in return.

And then Nikolaas was deposited next to us with no apparent grace or care for his survival.

"You, who speak as the fish do." A loud voice came from the dark. "Why do you shout at me with such anger?"

"It speaks?" I asked.

"That doesn't sound like speech." Eleanor grumbled.

"It may to her." Nikolaas said, trying to get himself standing, and falling over a few times.

"Why?" The voice implored.

"You are causing harm." I replied, taking a step towards the voice.

"All things cause harm. All things eat. All things die. This is not a reason." The voice retorted.

"Causing unnecessary harm is not what all things do." I took another step towards it.

"Do you honestly think you are a danger to me?" The darkness asked.

"Do you honestly think I care? You harmed the forest. You harmed my friend." I paused. "The townspeople are terrified because you have harmed them."

"And you have come to hunt me?" The darkness laughed. "You, Fish creature?"

My eyes focused intently, and the smells around me swirled with the unforgiving stench of demon flame.

It was my ears that gave the creature away. A heart beat.

I rushed towards it, but was met with a blast of fire.

I winced, and covered my face.

The fire stopped short.

"WHAT IS THIS?" The creature demanded.

I turned to look behind me.

Nikolaas held up a simple engraved rock.

It glowed a bright, almost ethereal blue.

"This." Nikolaas informed the dark. "Is magic."

There was a brief cut through the air before the creature screamed out in pain.

"And that." Nikolaas took a moment. "Was unexpected."

"That was an arrow." Eleanor said, helpfully.

"To the eye." I added, with a hungry grin. "Nice shot. My turn."

"Your turn for WHAT?" The darkness demanded. "You can't cause me any harm."

But I could smell the blood. I could hear the blood pumping.

I could smell the distress. My body was overtaken by familiar shark or wolf like instincts.

And then the creature dissolved into a pile of strange yellow powder, which I was unfortunately covered in.

I coughed out the foul tasting guck. At least it was not slime, but that didn't make it appetizing.

"What?" Nikolaas demanded. "Where did it go?"

"You do not belong." A quiet voice said from the bushes. "But you show spirit."

My nose flared. "Who are you?"

"I cannot give you my name." The creature replied.

"A fae? Great." I grumbled. "My day is going so cheery and bright."

"We are not they." The creature paused. "We are the keepers of the wild."

"The little people? The ones the innkeeper warned us about?" Nikolaas asked.

"One and the same. We do try to help your kind." There was a pause. "What business do you have, walking these roads when it is dangerous?"

"We hunt a creature who abducts children." I said, evenly.

"You hunt the *Krampus?*" The creature laughed heartily. "That sounds more stupid than hunting the Draeck."

"Hunters are not known for lacking stupidity." Nikolaas replied.

"You would insult yourself?" The creature asked.

"No. We explain ourselves. The creature hunts children. Our childhood was taken from us." Eleanor said softly.

"The night ahead is calm, now that the Draeck is felled." The creature paused. "Stay on the road. The night belongs to us."

"I can live with that arrangement." Nikolaas said, walking around the pile of yellow powder. "All things considered."

"First time I've seen a dragon killed." Eleanor said, looking at the powder with wonder.

"First time I've seen a *dragon*." Nikolaas retorted. "Though I've heard tales."

I remained silent.

"You?" The creature asked.

"They're a lot easier to kill when you can turn into a bat." My tone was intended to be informative. "They don't expect it. Being able to land on them and gouge their eyes is handy."

"You turned into a bat?" The creature paused. "You are not of the waters you are bound to. Your soul is ripped with magic."

"I haven't been human since I was seven years old." I informed it.

"Perhaps, not even then." The creature laughed. "Or if you were, that is long since lost. You have our condolences, Ocean hunter."

"That's precisely why I'm here." I laughed.

"We grant you permission. You may travel through our dark, mad hunters. But beware. That which you hunt is not of this realm." The creature began rustling away.

"Said the gnome to the woman currently cursed as a siren." I retorted.

There was a boisterous laugh as the creature departed.

"Well, damn." Nicholas took a seat in the snow. Curiously, he looked completely healed from his assault.

"What?" Eleanor implored.

"That thing just destroyed a dragon without so much as an implied effort." I filled in the gap.

"Oh." Eleanor blinked. "And it was afraid of the thing we hunt."

"We have it's name." Nicholas said, quietly.

"Is that important?" Eleanor looked suddenly hopeful.

"We can trap it, if we can find the right spell components." I looked out at the now peaceful dark.

The forest suddenly felt strangely welcoming and peaceful.

"How hard are they likely to be to find?" Eleanor said, running her finger through the yellow powder.

"An intended victim, something we can set alight, some chalk to draw some sigils, and most importantly, holly." Nikolaas said, thoughtfully. "I keep holly with me."

"Why?" I asked, confused by this admission.

"It protects." He laughed. "Even dragons don't like the smell of it. We have to wear some. It will stop the creature from killing us."

"That sounds slightly more important than the rest of the spell." Eleanor guessed.

"You would not be wrong." Nikolaas chuckled. "I am not particularly fond of ending up dead."

"How would you know?" Eleanor scrunched up her face.

"Hazard of the job." I grumbled. "I don't recommend it."

# The city of the waters

The city of Rotterdam was peaceful. Nothing quite so hushed or bewilderingly vacant as Beemer had been. The journey to get here after the first night was remarkably simple, despite taking several days, 3 different carriages and a boat.

We, the odd trio walked through the city, over varying bridges, pondering the place around us in silence.

For Eleanor, her silence was that of wonder. Rotterdam was quite a bit larger and more complex than Perrault. I had no real idea of what was going through the mind of our elderly guide, but mine was overflowing with strange smells and stranger thoughts.

The city smelled of bread, and cooking meats. Something possibly being roast vegetables, sewage, and a strong undercurrent of grime and mold.

My thoughts strayed from *that was a dragon* to *what the hell magic did Nikolaas use to ward off the dragon* and most importantly *what the hell had we gotten ourselves into?*

"Spare change?" A child asked as we walked past. I stopped to dig out a few pieces of silver and some bread that was nearly stale. The child looked quite grateful.

"A question, if I might." I asked. "Do you know of the being called *Krampus*?"

The child shifted uncomfortably, before nodding. "The orphanage. They are scared. It will come soon."

"Orphanage?" Nikolaas repeated for Eleanor. "That sounds... fortuitous."

"They're scared." Eleanor chastised him.

"We're here to kill it." I said, softly before switching back to Dutch. "Do you think you might lead us to the orphanage?"

The child looked bewildered at that.

"Nobody cares enough." The child said, quietly.

"To do what?" Nikolaas asked.

"Learn about it. Fight it. Kill it. Nothing. As far as most of the adults are concerned, it weeds down the orphanage, and roots out bad children. Saves on expenses." The child whispered. "So we behave. Most of us that are left, anyway."

"We care." I gave the child a reassuring smile. "We hunt monsters."

"The world has many." The child looked down. "Why care about this one?"

"Today, we care about it. Yesterday, a Draeck. A few months ago, a witch." I shook my head. "One day. One place. One Monster. We came here intending to do something else, but when we find trouble, we deal with it."

The child looked up, bewildered. "Draeck?"

Nikolaas inclined his head. "I've got the claw marks to prove it."

The child pondered this in silence. "I will take you to Mother Mary, but she may not have any interest in your help."

"Oh, I've never met a lady of the Christian cloth to turn down assistance when it costs nothing." Nikolaas replied.

"*Nothing*?" The child raised both of their eyebrows.

"The privilege to hunt a monster such as this is price enough." Nikolaas nodded.

"Come on." The child said, getting up and collecting their belongings.

"Always pays to spare a child a coin." I quietly said to Eleanor.

She tilted her head. "We've got a lead?"

"We have a trap." Nikolaas clarified.

"Now we just have to make sure to spring it before this thing kills any kids." I added.

"That sounds ominous." Eleanor looked at the child.

"I'm glad you understand." I laughed. "The kid told us that nobody cared about the thing enough to learn about it."

"Oh." Eleanor closed her eyes and scrunched up her face. "So we're fighting a mystery."

"It's just possible we can kill it, though. I did not fight it because I was informed we couldn't kill it." Nikolaas agreed. "The good part is that we know people just haven't bothered to learn and it may actually be possible. The bad part is that we still have no bloody idea how."

"Lovely." Eleanor grumbled.

# Cat and Mouse

The orphanage was cold and drafty. Almost every orphanage was. Nobody really cared enough to keep them up. Not like the churches that tended to run them.

Orphanages were places kids lived largely against their will.

That's also usually how money was spent on them.

This one was no different. The cold, damp winter chilled *nearly* everyone's bones.

Nikolas, Eleanor and I had the fortune of heavy cloaks, and in my case, an unnatural comfort in the cold.

Arranging things with the Mother Superior wasn't hard. Buying some extra food and firewood went far. The church always appreciated those who were kind to them. Especially with silver or gold. Didn't matter whose church. Any church of any faith, really.

Some of the children were settled next to the fire, within our chalk drawn magic circle, while Nikolas was telling tales of monsters and mischief.

Eleanor was enraptured with them, while also providing some stew.

I sat in the corner watching and listening. Waiting.

It was a simple plan. All we needed was to keep the children all together. And Alive.

And wait.

I hated this part. I quietly sipped ale. I sat. I waited.

This was part of the plan. I wasn't…

Normal.

By those who read souls. Nikolas, old. Eleanor, young and inexperienced.

My soul stunk of curse. Magic. Monsters.

I had to stay away from the children and the innocence, because it was a repellent to those who hunt those who are otherwise defenseless.

Monsters did, however, lurk in the dark, unseen by others all the time. That was sort of their life. Their home. It wasn't necessarily mine, but it was an expected place for me to be.

It was just the way of the world. Adapting to the situation. Camouflage by doing what was expected.

And so, here I waited.

The hairs on the back of my neck stood up, and I looked around, curious at what was causing it.

"Hello, my dear." A voice came from the shadows around me.

"I know you're here." I retorted. "You might as well show yourself."

The shadows coalesced into the vaguely sinister and shady form of my supposed benefactor, Rumpelstiltskin.

"You seem to take this personally, dear girl." Rumpelstiltskin noted, staring towards the collected group.

"I am them. They are me. They don't deserve what happened to me." I attempted a nonchalant shrug.

Rumpelstiltskin chuckled at that. "The world would be less dark, if you would show it how much you care."

"I doubt that. I'm just a girl from a backwater village who got bit by a werewolf, and decided to bite back." I laughed. It sounded so absurd.

Rumpelstiltskin shook his head. "This version of our world reflects the magic we put into it. You chose to care. Look at the results."

Eleanor's golden hair flashed and flickered with the reflected flames of the fireplace, and my brooding irritation was replaced by a calmer smile.

Then, I froze. "What do you mean, this version?"

"There was once another. A man wanted power. He took it. He plunged the world into this magical alteration." Rumpelstiltskin frowned, and tilted his head. "This is a symptom. You begin to understand after a while. Magic doesn't belong here."

I was silent for some time, sipping from my flask. I stared at Eleanor in thought.

"That's why you are helping me." My voice grew softer so that others couldn't overhear.

Rumpelstiltskin inclined his head. "I've done it before. Cleopatra helped, once. She was a feisty one. Can't believe I married her." His mood changed to something closer to melancholy. "She was nothing like Nefirtiti. Or Sigyn." He closed his eyes, then smiled. "Or Angrboda."

He shook his head. "No matter. Reminiscent moments aren't moments such as these. I'm here to hunt this thing with you. He won't like the idea, so I've hung back."

"Why?" Whenever I asked this question, it seemed to imply so much more than just a request for an answer.

Rumpelstiltskin drew in the air, and glowing green runes traced along as his fingers went.

"There was a man who stole me once, and called me his son." Rumpelstiltskin stared at the runes in silence. "After a time, he and my adoptive brother killed my children. All of them. They are gone. The ones I've loved are gone."

He closed his eyes. "Everything is gone except anger." He reached for my flask.

I handed it to him, wordlessly.

"Warm hearths and full bellies." He raised the flask.

"You want this thing dead because you hate what it does to children. You see it, and see your adoptive father reflected." I said, holding a hand out into the light, and allowing webbing to form between the fingers.

Rumpelstiltskin held his hand into the light and it turned a frosty blue.

"To save my people, I imprisoned them in a realm of shadow with stolen magic, and left my daughter's spirit to guard it. That's what I do. I steal magic." He said, handing my webbed hand my flask back, with his blue one. "In her name, it was thus called the shadow realm of Helheim. That magic wasn't all that different than the magic that is folded into this world."

His hand returned a pale olive. "But now, because your world and it's magic have collided once more, the path to Helheim is accessible. That's not great for either side of that path. Nor, for that matter, either side of the veil between your worlds."

"In what sense-?" I cut myself off. "Magic destroyed my life and I made it my mission to destroy it back."

"The Jotun as a people are about as warm and welcoming as the frigid air creaking through the rafters." Rumpelstiltskin took a moment. "What's terrifying about your world is how astonishingly snow white they pale in comparison to the creatures your world has brought into existence."

"Can we stop it?" It was such a simple question, once again.

"Yes." Rumpelstiltskin chuckled. "Yes, we can. But we have to weaken it first. The things like this are sort of guardians, or anti-seals. They leak too much magic into your world to allow it to close."

"And it's been closed before." I added.

"Egyptian folklore certainly makes dragons look cheery and bright, but yes. It can be done. If the creatures leaking a great deal of magic into your world are killed. You've already started." Rumpelstiltskin withdrew a pipe from seemingly nowhere and took a long drag off of it.

"The fairy?" I asked.

Rumpelstiltskin nodded. "The fairy. The boss fairy. Fairy God-mothers are usually the first to be able to breach the veil. Though that wasn't the case in Egypt, let me tell you something, Nefirtiti had to invent words to express herself after facing some of your Celtic beasts. They wouldn't translate but I'm sure you could grasp the idea."

"I think I'd have liked her." I took a sip from my flask.

"You two together would be the eleventh plague of Egypt. That girl knew how to fight, and she knew how to have a good time in equal measure." Rumpelstiltskin's laughter drew Eleanor's attention, but she returned her attention to the kids shortly after.

"This thing is the antithesis to a good time." He added, staring towards the fireplace.

"You have stopped charging for such information, then?" I inquired.

Rumpelstiltskin shrugged. "Some jobs you do for the peace of the child nobody else cares about."

"And who taught you that?" I asked, bemused.

"You did." He shrugged. "All throughout the world, there are celebrations on the solstice, or thereabouts. A jubilation of being halfway through the harshest darks, and colds. Closer to the warmth, the food to be grown, and the end of the biting chill. These celebrations did just one thing wrong. They demonized the cold and the dark. The frost that sucks the life from your soul. They created a figure of winter, darker than coal, and hungrier than the angriest of wolves." He looked up at the hole filled rafters. "And this thing decided it liked living, as all living things do. There was a time that sacrifices were made to appease it in different places. For a time, that was enough. Until a nobleman who was obsessed with retaining his youth decided to kill bothersome children. He was hung, and his soul hit the veil. It was stolen by this darkness on the day of his death. Now, they serve each other. Once a year, he steals the sacrifices needed for the dark and the dark in turn gives him a year as a child, himself. The theft of youth, and the empowerment of evil."

"If I know my curses, and I like to think I do, given that I'm one of the world's premier curse masters, that means he likely strikes first at the time he was hanged." I pointed out.

"Sundown." Rumpelstiltskin paused. "In this town, no less."

There was a silence between us as the last bits of sunlight began to fade from view through the disheveled rafters.

"Get ready." Rumpelstiltskin said, quietly.

I drew my silver sword with caution.

Taking my cue, Eleanor grabbed hers, then Nikolas, his axe.

He looked towards me, then the man waiting alongside me, and he frowned.

The fire went out in the fireplace.

"It begins." Rumpelstiltskin said, quietly.

He drew four runes in the air, and each one landed on either himself, myself, Eleanor or Nikolas, and was then mirrored onto a child.

"What the HEL are you doing?" Nikolas demanded.

"Where they go, we go. You'd better get ready." Rumpelstiltskin laughed.

"YOU TREACHEROUS SNAKE, YOU'LL GET US KILLED!" Nikolas shouted.

"HAZARD OF THE JOB!" Rumpelstiltskin retorted.

There was a dark laugh.

The children were absconded through some kind of misty portal carried by a creature on it's back.

And then, thin green lines formed between the portal and the four of us, and we were sucked through green portals mimicking the portal of dark.

# The isle of despair

(act two)

## Lost boys (and girls to promote gender equality and avoid copyright issues)

The moon greeted the four as the first thing we could see. We were lying on our backs, staring up.

"How did we get here, exactly?" Eleanor asked, not bothering to get up just yet.

"Treachery." Nikolas grumbled. "Why would you travel with THAT fiend?"

"Charming." Rumpelstiltskin noted, brushing himself up, then helping Eleanor up.

I got up, and bared my less human teeth at the place around us.

"Something wrong?" Eleanor asked in an almost rhetorical sense.

"This place. It reeks of magic." I narrowed my eyes at Nikolas. "And I don't recall you having any plans to actually get here, so it's probably best not to insult the person who has our metaphorical horses that we need to leave this place locked in their stable."

Nikolas took a swing at Rumpelstiltskin, apparently not convinced by my suggestion.

I caught his fist.

"ENOUGH!" I shouted loudly enough to cause him to stagger back and cover his ears. Siren shouts could be very unpleasant above the water. I was getting very comfortable with how things reacted to them. It was instinct, now.

"I don't care about you, and I don't care about him." Eleanor added, shoving Nikolas backwards. "In case you forgot, there were kids abducted to this place by a nefarious dark dwelling creature who intends to *eat* them."

Nikolas opened his mouth.

I dug my claws into his arm.

"Alright, alright!" Nikolas held up his other hand. "For now, any-way."

Rumpelstiltskin shook his head and looked around us. My atten-tion likewise wandered, once I let go of Nikolas' arm.

We had apparently landed at the edge of a beach. There was a small cove inside, and my attention was drawn to it, for some reason. Not quite a scent. Something sharper.

Rumpelstiltskin's attention was similarly drawn, and he grabbed both Eleanor and Nikolas, and pulled them back. "I think this is your dance, my dear girl."

I nodded, and stepped forward, permitting much of my body to curse shift. "I can't see you but I know you're here." My words didn't seem to go far, but blonde and orange hair popped out of the cove, and eyes that didn't quite reflect the moonlight as human eyes did greeted my voice.

"You do not speak our language." One of the sirens said in a raspy version of English.

This unsettled me more than anything else, and Nikolas and Rum-pelstiltskin both seemed surprised, though Eleanor just looked confused.

"How is it that you speak these words?" I asked, my own tongue returning to English.

"They're speaking French." Eleanor replied.

"They're speaking all-speech." Rumpelstiltskin corrected. "Which makes them unique, indeed."

"Much like your snake tongued friend." Nikolas agreed.

"Why have you come here, you of mortal souls?" The other siren asked, looking at Eleanor and Nikolas.

"To kill the child stealer." Eleanor replied, tilting her head. "Strange. I always assumed sirens were impossible to resist."

"They are." Nikolas retorted.

"Unless you're a siren, a god, or one of an assortment of cursed creatures." Rumpelstiltskin added.

"Or marked by one of us as their own." The first siren tilted her head. "How curious. To see one of our kind with one of yours." They focused their attention on me. "You were one of hers, once."

I nodded. "A very long time ago."

"Your soul sings of us,  now. You have hunted as we hunt, and killed as we killed. We do not cause harm to those like us." They focused on Nikolas. "Nor do we ensnare men who treat women with kindness."

Their attention focused on Rumpelstiltskin. "As to you." The second frowned. "We may be many things, but we would not accost a soul as in pain as yours unless provoked. We could soothe it, if you wished."

"I do not." Rumpelstiltskin shook his head. "Though it's a kind offer."

"Did you just try to seduce the God of Lies and Treachery?" Nikolas looked surprised.

The first hissed. "We care not for such petty titles. We care only about the pain."

The second nodded. "We come to this place to stop that which dwells here from taking immortal children. Were we able to kill him, he would be dead. What he does is not the way things should be done."

"You're lucky we don't show you how things should be done-" Nikolas began.

My sword was at his throat.

He winced.

"Sirens are rarely monsters as the bards claim. If you were any kind of huntsman worth his salt, you would know that they cannot stand the pain of a tormented soul." I interrupted. "You may keep your ill informed preconceptions to yourself, because if you utter a single other fell word about these women, or by extension, me, I will leave your body here, and let your soul move on. You haven't particularly done much of use. The term dead-weight can become literal, should you continue."

Nikolas took a step back, and inclined his head.

"Forgive my companion. He is not as well travelled as the bards claim." I added.

"They really are like us." Eleanor said, moving closer to the shoreline, and taking them in better.

"They live in a world where you eat, or you are eaten. It is rare for kindness to be offered." Rumpelstiltskin agreed. "They may have full bellies, but you'll not find too many who have ever known peace or an equivalent to a warm hearth."

"Barring the royal family." The second siren hissed. "How do you intend to get the children out of this place?"

"I hadn't actually got quite that far in the plan." Rumpelstiltskin said, looking surprised by the topic shift.

"Plan?" Eleanor laughed.

"We will aid." The first nodded. "Consider it a recompense for your services."

Nikolas nodded, and Eleanor looked a bit relieved but I exchanged a look with Rumpelstiltskin.

"What service?" I implored, looking surprised by both their under-standing of human compensation for work, and their need for our services.

"In order to keep the children safe, we cannot leave this place." The second siren looked down. "There was once a third. She left with some of the children and did not return."

"You are the first that we have witnessed come here by magic not of that creature." The first added.

"Technically, it was." Rumpelstiltskin laughed. "Though it was a mimicry, not the actual act."

"And you cannot easily do so again." She guessed.

"I absolutely could." Rumpelstiltskin paused. "But curiously, I'm having to use most of my powers just to keep these two alive."

"The island of the dark draws life force from mortal souls." The second nodded. "If you can prevent that, it is likely that you will be very much restrained by this place."

"What of our own magic?" Nikolas asked.

The first scrunched up her face. "I do not like this one. He is as good at hunting as a deaf dolphin." She shook her head. "Unless it is magic of this place, or powerful magic, it will only be absorbed by this place, and make it stronger."

"Veil magic will sort of work. Shadow magic only sort of works." Rumpelstiltskin paused. "Deity magic would work. But not more generic human magic."

"Precisely." The mermaid tilted her head. "You know of the veil. Fascinating."

"Should he not?" Eleanor asked.

"Now that it has meshed with your world, no." The second laughed. "We thought humans had forgotten."

"He's not exactly from around Earth." Nikolas corrected.

"Where, then?" The first looked at Rumpelstiltskin, raising what passed for eyebrows on her hairless head.

"I am from a place called Jotunheim, though I was raised on Asgard." Rumpelstiltskin narrowed his eyes at her.

"Ice child?" The siren looked bewildered. "How fascinating. We thought your kind were gone."

"They are." He looked away.

The second looked towards the island. "Follow the only star. You will find the children."

"And if you attempt to take them, he will stop you." The first added. "We grieve with you, Loki of Jotunheim." She looked down at the moon's reflection on the water. "We know something of what it is to lose our kind."

"You do?" Eleanor frowned.

"There are so few left." The second closed her eyes. "The world hunts us, wanting us gone because of the few of our kind who hunt the humans."

"And the supposed King does nothing." The first looked very irritated. "We are what is left of our kind. And our sister, if she still remains. Those of us who can cast the magic of the veil are the heaviest hunted. As are the seawitch folk who taught us."

"I am sorry." Eleanor tilted her head. "Is that how you can speak to each of us in our own language?"

"You are very wise." The second nodded. "It is not all-speech."

"Magic speech?" Rumpelstiltskin laughed. "That's parlor tricks. You should-"

He paused, coming to the obvious realization at the same time that I did.

"You can't do much else." I interjected. "Because you have to conserve your energies to protect those who are trapped here."

"We always fail." The first one looked at me, narrowing her eyes on mine. "But I see eyes that are not of us, nor of your companions. You hunt with the hunger of a shark, and the teeth of something far more terrifying. Whatever corrupted your soul might just be enough."

"That's a nice compliment." Nikolas shook his head. "It's not like she had a choice."

"It actually is a compliment." Rumpelstiltskin chastised.

"I haven't been human since I was seven." I agreed. "It's occasionally nice to have my abilities actually respected."

Eleanor looked towards the star. She looked towards the pitch black sky around it.

"That star follows the children?" Eleanor asked.

The first siren shook her head. "It casts light on exactly one place on this island. The creature keeps the children there, so that they don't try to seek out things in the forest like us."

"Or worse." The second laughed. "Though I wouldn't worry. Three of you are far more terrifying than what's in there, and the old man smells very unappetizing."

"That's absolutely charming." Nikolas crossed his arms and turned away.

"It's not inaccurate." I retorted. "Thank you for your help. I would ask your names, if you would oblige. I understand if you cannot offer them."

"I am Genevieve." The orange haired one looked towards Nikolas. "She will not introduce herself in front of him, however."

"Why not?" Nikolas demanded.

"Because I do not like you." The first shrugged.

Nikolas didn't say anything. He just walked towards the forest.

"I am Rachel of Dresmoor. This is Eleanor Tremaine." I said, quietly. "And we appreciate your assistance."

"For one of the last of our sisters?" The brunette smiled. "I am grateful for the opportunity. I am called Aurellia. Should you find yourself in need of aid, when you leave this place, my family will assist you."

"Thank you." Eleanor tilted her head. "Do you think something's wrong with him?" She inclined her head towards the forest.

"He smells of death, yet his soul clings to mortality." Aurellia looked confused. "He does not belong to this place, nor yours. Something haunts him."

"*He* haunts him." Genevieve corrected.

"The forests don't like him either." I looked from the forest to Rumpelstiltskin. "And if this one knows, he's not talking."

"Considering where he hails from, I am not surprised." Rumpelstiltskin shook his head. "Those who live as he has do not go quietly into the night."

"I imagine that if he did not have your protections, he would not suffer much ill in this place." Genevieve shook her head. "I doubt death, herself, could take him from that body."

"Death is a woman?" Eleanor looked surprised.

Rumpelstiltskin snorted. "It depends on which Death."

"What do you mean, which death?"

"Last time, his name was Osiris. Good fellow, actually."

# The again walker and the eater of children

The circle in the forest that the children were kept in felt ethereal. There was a strange magic at play that made my bones chill.

The children were crying, and huddled together. They stopped crying when they saw Eleanor.

We approached the children, and a shadow stepped between us.

It took the form of a darkened part ox, part man.

It's eyes were red, and it did not look impressed.

I wasn't, either. It was using parlor tricks to appear as a religious figure that supposedly was the antithesis to the Christian god of creation. As one who had no use for religion, I found it little more than irritating.

"You do not belong here." The creature hissed.

"Pietr." Nikolas stared down the creature. "You do not belong here, either."

The creature stared at Nikolas for a moment, bewildered. "Nobody has called me that in a long time."

"It is your name, after all." Rumpelstiltskin countered. "Pan player, if I'm not mistaken. Quite the actor in your time, as well. Not sure how he knew your-"

The creature lunged at Rumpelstiltskin, and Rumpelstiltskin parried with a knife. The knife dissolved into the shadow, and when he pulled his hand back, it was empty and bright blue.

Nikolas, apparently finding some tiny mote of courage, swung his axe at the creature. It went clean through the creature, but what came out of the creature was a broken handle and no axe head.

Eleanor readied her blade, but I held up my hand.

I twirled the silver sword that I could still wield, and swung at the creature. It went through him, but remained intact.

"That axe was made of iron, just as your sword." Nikolas explained. "It'd do no good to waste your weapon."

The creature lunged towards Eleanor, but I jumped into its way and screamed loudly. The creature staggered back.

I fell to the ground as well, and my belongings scattered around me. I stood up, and brushed myself off.

The creature lunged at Nikolas, next. Nikolas' form stayed still, but a rotting skeleton fell out from it, behind him.

Nikolas screamed a terrifying banshee scream, and the creature staggered back once more.

He fell back onto the skeleton, then stood again, apparently absorbing it.

"Lich." I said, quietly. "How clever."

"Draugr. Technically." Rumpelstiltskin corrected. "Liches don't tend to be able to maintain their human form like that. You ought to know, yes?"

I shot him a dirty look.

"What?" Eleanor scrunched up her face.

"A spirit that refuses to die." Nikolas said, punching the creature, and knocking it backwards. "Bound to the body that was once its own."

"That's only slightly creepy." Eleanor said, moving to hide behind me.

"Get the children to the bay." I instructed.

The star grew brighter and the forest dimmed out.

"You cannot leave." The creature laughed. "Once you are here, you are here."

Rumpelstiltskin looked around, and raised his eyebrows.

"What?" Nikolas asked, looking towards him with a curious look.

"You remember how I told you that I was being drained by protecting you and her?" Rumpelstiltskin asked.

Nikolas looked towards the creature, and struck him again. No change of result. Perhaps thinking was not his strong suit, either. It was actually getting tedious.

"What kind of wood is your axe handle made of?" Eleanor asked from behind me.

"Pine. Why?" Nikolas asked.

I turned. She had picked up one of the magic books from my bag.

Rumpelstiltskin smiled. "Thank goodness we brought the clever one."

"You can't defeat me." The creature said, narrowing its eyes at Eleanor.

"Oh. Of course not." Rumpelstiltskin chuckled. "But there's something we can do."

"I was human, once." I added.

The creature looked at me with uncertainty. "You are of the tide-walkers. While they amuse me, you should not jest."

"I'm not." I paused. "I was made into one."

Eleanor began muttering something. The area around us began to shift. It turned very cold, as though it were tuning into the seasons of the world we had been ripped from.

The creature staggered back and hissed.

"Pietr pan player." Eleanor held the book out towards him. "You wanted to be like this."

"Why can I not..." The creature looked confused. It touched one of the children but was repulsed as though its hand was burned. It screamed an unpleasant sound that nearly matched my siren screen.

"The curse comes with a fun little bit that prevents magic from changing you from what you are turned into." I explained, trying to keep the creature's attention off of Nikolas.

Nikolas was sharpening the end of what was previously his axe. He had managed to grasp enough of what was going on to understand why Eleanor needed to know what the handle was made of.

The creature hissed at me and Eleanor. Eleanor hissed back. I simply glared at it.

And then there was a sound. A sickly, sucking sound. The creature exploded into black goop, and I spat some of the foul slime out of my mouth.

Now also covered in black, Nikolas and Rumpelstiltskin exchanged irritated looks, while Nikolas held up his stick.

"Pine." Nikolas said, after a moment. "Very clever, that." He began to flicker out. "What-?"

# The Klaas Clause

The slime was not easy to get off, but what was more concerning to me was how it was affecting Nikolas. His spirit seemed to be unable to keep hold of its body, now that it was covered in this slime.

The black covered skeleton fell from him in a pile.

"We can't just leave those here." Rumpelstiltskin frowned. "You'll never be able to leave this place."

"I already can't." Nikolas said, quietly. "I can feel it. The call of the cold. The pull of the dark. I can't seem to connect to my body. I'm cold."

"That's a clever trick, that." Rumpelstiltskin poked the black goop on his arm. He snapped his finger, and he and I were clean, but the goop did not leave Nikolas' bones.

"It's bonded to his body." Eleanor frowned. "This is the stuff that made Krampus what he was. Forever stuck here."

The forest returned around us, and I looked at the children. "Eleanor, see if you can get a fire started from those trees. The kids can't handle this cold for long."

Eleanor nodded, and headed into the brush. She returned with an armful of branches in a matter of minutes. "The woods are falling apart."

"This place is dying." Nikolas shook his head. "We won't be able to get to the bay in time. I can feel it. Without the ability to absorb from the children, it is faltering."

I picked up one of the spellbooks from my bag. I looked around thoughtfully.

"Fairies function on belief. What if…" I trailed off.

"What if is good." Rumpelstiltskin prodded. "What if… what?"

"What if we curse this place to function on the belief of children in some sort of guardian?" I asked.

"And let the old man retire?" Eleanor asked. "What would you do if you weren't killing monsters?"

Nikolas looked at the children, and smiled at their joy at the fire. "I suppose I'd want to see the kids safe, happy and smiling."

"Make them toys." A voice said, from the woods.

"What?" Rumpelstiltskin turned towards the forest, squinting.

"Don't look." I instructed, having recognized the voice. "They don't take kindly. We must be phasing out, allowing the real world to bleed in."

"Right you are, cursed huntswoman." The voice laughed. "You have done the impossible, but yet you still seek a way to help the children. We will help you, Nikolas Klaas. We will help you craft toys for the children, and once a year, on the darkest night, you will bring all the children toys, and this place will continue. You will continue. And your companions may leave. We take this place as our own."

"Unseen by all but one." Eleanor added.

"An acceptable arrangement." Nikolas nodded.

"I require the book." The voice noted.

I closed my eyes and counted my steps as I walked into the woods. I placed the book in the snow and stepped back the exact same number of steps.

When I opened my eyes, the book was gone.

The forest dissolved as strange words echoed through the air around us and a wooden house sprung up around the fire.

The goop around Nikolas' bones burned red, before it and they dissolved altogether.

His once blue robe turned a similar shade of red.

"As we promised." Nikolas said, kneeling next to the children. "You are all safe."

The children began to smile, and the house lit up.

"You must leave, now." A voice came from a shadow that was cast in the corner.

"Come along." Eleanor said, gently escorting the children out.

Where there was once a bewildering to navigate forest, now there was a stone path. We followed it to the frozen shores.

The children sang happy songs as we walked.

The darkened night lit up with new stars, and green, red, and blue ribbons streaked through the skies.

When we got to the bay, there was no one present, but there was a swirling vortex at the end of the path.

# The lightless solstice

Time had passed in an unusual fashion, and when we were deposited back in the rivers of Rotterdam, thankfully with boats to contain us as we landed, there was a distinct feeling of relief.

"In the end, he was brave." Eleanor said, quietly.

"One last huzzah." I agreed.

Rumpelstiltskin didn't say anything. He just tied the boats to the shore.

We helped the children back to the orphanage, to the shock of the mother superior.

"You've been gone for nearly a week!" She exclaimed.

"Seemed a lot shorter to us." Rumpelstiltskin said, in as cryptic a tone as he could muster.

She knelt down and hugged one of the children who ran up to her.

We helped the old nun get the kids all inside, and were surprised to be greeted by a pine tree decorated with candles and toys sitting in the middle of the main room by the fire.

The nun, in particular, had the most flabbergasted expression. "That wasn't here just minutes ago."

One of the children walked up to the tree, and their eyes went wide. "Mother superior, this one has my name on it!"

A quick examination of the tree revealed that each toy had a specific child's name on it, and every single child in the orphanage had one.

The children began to laugh, and play with their newfound toys.

"Well, that's a perfectly acceptable resolution." The old nun held out three silver pieces.

Eleanor and I shook our heads at the same time. One of the children brought us each a toy with our names engraved on them. A ballerina and a replica of Nikolas' axe.

"We have been paid." Rumpelstiltskin said, looking at the tree. It had one last toy on it.

A small spinning wheel.

And on the bottom, etched into the wood, were three words.

*That tricky bastard.*

Rumpelstiltskin spun the wheel and began to laugh.

The ribbons of red, green, and blue streaked across the sky in this world, too. Visible through the cracks in the roof, they were a breath-taking sight.

"On the darkest of nights, no less." The nun said, looking up at the strange patterns, and laughing. "Well, I'll be."

Songs began to fill the streets outside, and we stepped out the door to listen better.

"What are they singing about?" Eleanor asked.

"Tidings of comfort and joy." I replied, with a smirk.

I turned to Rumpelstiltskin.

He was gone.

The spinning wheel sat on the floor, still spinning.

I picked it up and spun it thoughtfully.

"I suppose you'll be off now. People to save, and all that." The nun said, looking at the spinning wheel. "Disappearing into the night as he did."

"Not quite." I shook my head, and held up the toy axe. "We can stay a bit." I added in French, for Eleanor.

"What? Really?" Eleanor looked surprised.

"Do you know one of the first things they teach a huntsman?" I asked her.

"No." Eleanor shook her head.

I held up the toy axe, and smiled.

# The woodswoman's wish

## (epilogue)

# *Axes and wooden hammers*

Occasionally, the nuns would bring us warm broth or tea. They appreciated what we were doing, and food and lodging was perfectly fine payment as far as either of us were concerned.

We sat upon the roof, replacing the rotted beams as we went.

Eleanor looked absolutely delighted. Her father, after all, had been a smith. To be taught how to properly hew, treat, and then assemble a roof's worth of wood was something her father had never been permitted to teach her.

She didn't stop smiling the entire two weeks that we spent fixing the roof, cold be damned.

After the job was done, we spent one last night at the church.

"It's warmer, but the view is less enticing." Eleanor said, looking up at the rafters of the orphanage.

"We appreciate it." One of the nuns noted in French. "It will save on fuel for the fires." She added in Dutch.

"And we will not have to empty buckets of rain water." The mother superior added.

"Are you certain that you don't require payment for that?" The nun asked.

I shook my head. "I don't think you quite understand."

"What?" The mother superior asked.

"Eleanor wanted to see something she had never seen before. We spent two weeks drinking tea, eating your wonderful soup, and doing something she had never done. We have seen things that even I haven't seen before." I shook my head. "We wanted time away from hunting. To be at peace for a short while."

"And?" The nun asked.

"And I don't think I've ever been quite as much at peace, as I was, watching her smile while we fixed that roof." I explained. "You gave me a wish fulfilled. To see her no longer sad, nor resentful of those who had caused her harm."

"I do not think you can pay someone anything more fulfilling than that." The mother superior inclined her head, before leaving to check on the children.

I looked at Eleanor and a gentle smile returned to my face. "More precious than any amount of silver or gold."

Eleanor looked towards me with a curious look. "Is everything alright?"

"I don't think I could ask for anything more." I replied, sitting down next to her, and wrapping her under my cloak.

"Anything more than what?" She looked even more confused.

"Than to see you, no matter how briefly, robbed of the dark that causes you so much pain." I rested my head against hers.

"I was thinking much the same, actually." She took a sip of her tea. "You don't seem so cursed, or angry anymore."

"For now." I shrugged.

"For now?" She looked at me, confusion returning to her face.

"Such is the life we choose. There will undoubtedly be something to curse us or piss us off in the future. We tend to go looking for trouble. Sort of the job description." I scrunched up my face and bonked my nose against hers. "Though I will say, I forgot what moments like this were like."

"That's terrible." She looked slightly sad at that. "These are the moments you're fighting for, after all."

I closed my eyes and rested my forehead against hers.

"Yes." I said, quietly. "Yes, they are."

~*Fin*~

*Rachel Hood, Eleanor Tremain,*
*and Rumpelstiltskin will return in*

## Red Hood Rising: The Black Forest

-

May your shoe have a juicy
mandarin and your heart be fulfilled
with all the chocolate you desire.

Happy halfway out of the dark
from Frosted Siren Books.

9 798784 964045